by
Alison McGhee

illustrated by
Ross MacDonald

A Paula Wiseman Book
Simon & Schuster Books for Young Readers
New York London Toronto Sydney

SIMON & SCHUSTER BOOKS FOR YOUNG READERS
An imprint of Simon & Schuster Children's Publishing Division
1230 Avenue of the Americas, New York, New York 10020
Text copyright © 2008 by Alison McGhee
Illustrations copyright © 2008 by Ross MacDonald
All rights reserved, including the right of reproduction in whole or in part in any form.
SIMON & SCHUSTER BOOKS FOR YOUNG READERS is a trademark of Simon & Schuster.
Book design by Einav Aviram
The text for this book is set in Mc Kracken.
The illustrations for this book are rendered in watercolors and pencil crayon,
with some letterpress wood type.
Manufactured in China
10 9 8 7 6 5 4 3 2 1
Library of Congress Cataloging-in-Publication Data
McGhee, Alison, 1960–
Bye-bye, crib / Alison McGhee : illustrated by Ross MacDonald. – 1st ed.
p. cm.
"A Paula Wiseman book."
Summary: A big boy and his best stuffed friend seek the courage to move to a gigantic
new bed.
ISBN-13: 978-1-4169-1621-5 (hardcover)
ISBN-10: 1-4169-1621-0 (hardcover)
[1. Beds–Fiction. 2. Growth–Fiction.] I. MacDonald, Ross, 1957– ill. II. Title.
PZ7.M4784675By 2007
[E]–dc22
2006010583

To my nieces and nephews: Charlotte Reine
Steiner, William Chiva Blackett, Donald Chivorn
Blackett, McGhee Louise Steiner, Marshall
Washington Steiner, and Evan Caniglia McGhee,
and also to Aunt Judy Schiller

                                        –A. M.

For Quilty and Froggy

                                        –R. M.

This is me.   And this is Baby Kitty.

Pleased to meet you!

I'm a big boy now.
You know what
that means.

No bottle.

No diaper.

And lots of muscles.   Right, Baby Kitty?

Yes, I'm a big boy now.
And big boys sleep in big beds.
Here's what Mom and Dad say:

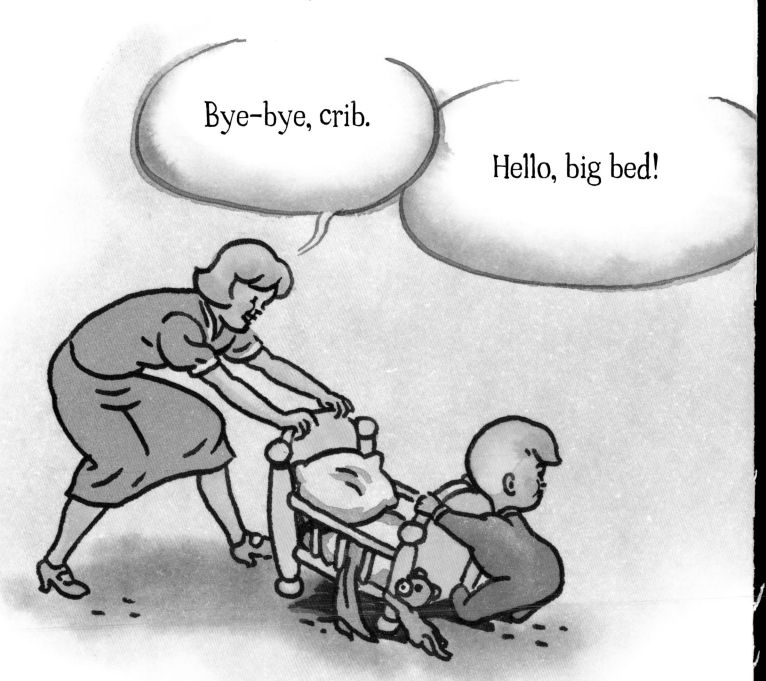

Here's what Baby Kitty and I say:

Not every big boy wants to sleep in a big bed.

I'll show you why.
Take a look at that big bed.
That one right over there.

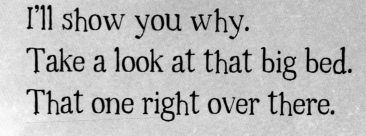

See what I mean?
That's not a big bed.
That's a monster bed.

Do big boys have to
sleep in monster beds?

Here's what Baby Kitty and I say:

Here's what Mom and Dad say:

Even if it wants to eat me alive?

Be brave.

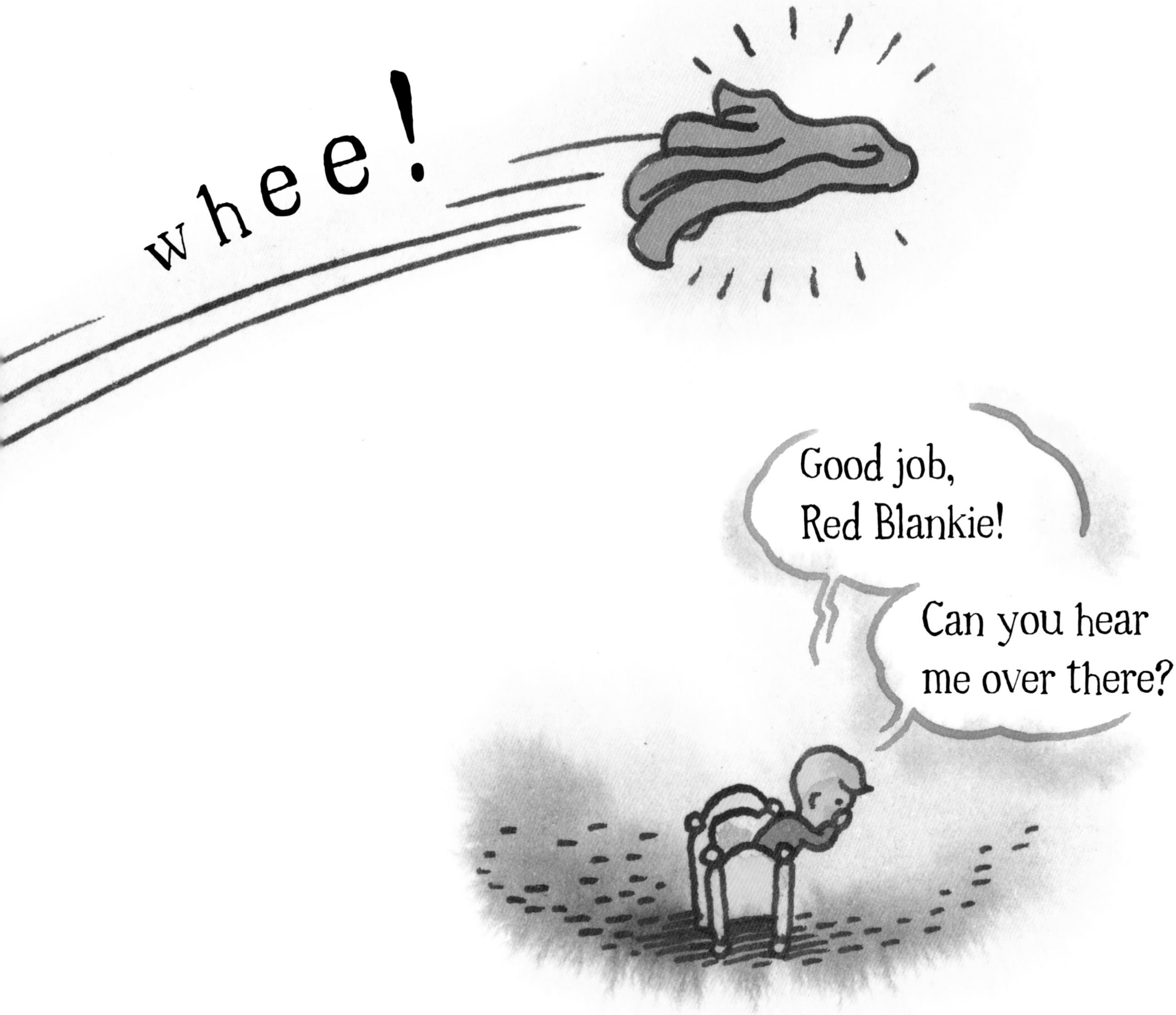
whee!
Good job,
Red Blankie!
Can you hear
me over there?

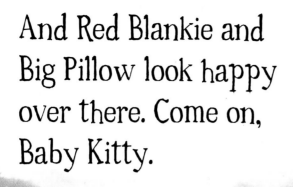

And Red Blankie and Big Pillow look happy over there. Come on, Baby Kitty.

Let's hold paws. You're safe with the muscle boy. Are you ready?

Here's what Baby Kitty and I say:

Muscle cats and muscle boys sleep in big beds.

Like this one.

This one right here.